Gold Rush Winter

by Claire Rudolf Murphy
illustrated by Richard Waldrep

A STEPPING STONE BOOK™
Random House New York

To my dear friend Jane Haigh, who has
helped me uncover the stories in history
—C.R.M.

Text copyright © 2002 by Claire Rudolf Murphy. Illustrations copyright © 2002 by Richard Waldrep. All rights reserved under International and Pan-American Copyright Conventions. Published in the United States by Random House Children's Books, a division of Random House, Inc., New York, and simultaneously in Canada by Random House of Canada Limited, Toronto. Originally published by Golden Books, an imprint of Random House Children's Books, a division of Random House, Inc., New York, in 2002.

www.randomhouse.com/kids

Library of Congress Cataloging-in-Publication Data
Murphy, Claire Rudolf.
Gold rush winter / by Claire Rudolf Murphy ; illustrated by Richard Waldrep. — 1st Random House ed.
    p. cm. "A Stepping Stone book."
SUMMARY: At the end of the nineteenth century, Swedish Americans Klondy and her mother travel from South Dakota to Alaska to live with Klondy's father, a gold miner who left for the mines when she was just a baby. Based on events in the life of Klondy Nelson.
ISBN 0-307-26413-0 (trade) — ISBN 0-307-46413-X (lib. bdg.)
1. Nelson, Klondy, b. 1897—Juvenile fiction. [1. Nelson, Klondy, b. 1897—Fiction.
2. Gold mines and mining—Fiction. 3. Fathers and daughters—Fiction.
4. Alaska—History—19th century—Fiction. 5. Swedish Americans—Fiction.]
I. Waldrep, Richard, ill. II. Title.
PZ7.M95155Go 2005
[Fic]—dc22 2003025398

First Random House Edition
Printed in the United States of America   11 10 9 8 7 6 5 4 3 2

RANDOM HOUSE and colophon are registered trademarks and A STEPPING STONE BOOK and colophon are trademarks of Random House, Inc.

Contents

1. North to Gold Country!   1

2. By Horse and by Husky   10

3. The Cabin at Ophir Creek   18

4. Papa Gets Angry   24

5. Klondy's Christmas   33

    Author's Note   44

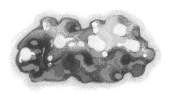

1

North to Gold Country!

Every night in Blacktail Gulch, South Dakota, I said my prayers and stared at Papa's photograph.

My papa was a miner. When I was a tiny baby, he set off to look for gold in the Far North. I didn't know the sound of his voice. I didn't know the feel of his scratchy beard. I didn't even know what it was like to spend Christmas with him.

Papa gave me my name—Klondy. He named me after the Klondike Gold Rush of 1897. That's where Papa went. He hoped to strike it rich in the Yukon Territory. It was thousands of miles north in Canada. Every few months a letter came. But never my papa. And never any money.

After Papa went away, Mama and I lived at a boardinghouse. Mama made Swedish pancakes and meatballs for the boarders. She had learned to cook them in Sweden when she was a little girl. I always wished Mama and I could cook for Papa instead.

Then one fall day, when I came home from school, Mama wore the biggest smile I'd ever seen.

"Klondy, your papa has moved to a new gold camp. It's near Nome, Alaska," she said, hugging me. "He sent us money to join him."

"Papa wants us to come?" I whispered. I was happy. But I also felt scared. Alaska was so far away.

"Finally we will be a family," Mama told me.

"Oh, Mama," I said. I didn't know if

I was laughing or crying. I was going to gold country!

Mama kept me so busy, I had no time to worry. We packed our belongings. We bought warm clothes for the trip. We said good-bye to our friends.

A train took us to Seattle. There we boarded a huge steamer ship. It traveled north to Alaska. Mama and I walked the deck. The weather was getting colder. Big icebergs drifted in the ocean.

After ten long days, the captain called out, "Land ho!" I ran down the gangplank as soon as the ship docked.

The men all had whiskers. They all wore plaid shirts. But no one looked like Papa's photograph.

Because of the big gold strike, I had thought Nome would be like a fairy tale with streets paved in gold. Nome wasn't like my dream at all. It had muddy roads and rows of dirty white tents. And no Papa in sight.

A little man came over. "You must be Klondy," he said. "I'm Blueberry Pete. I'm your papa's partner."

"I thought Papa would meet us here." I blinked so the tears wouldn't come.

"Your papa's busy digging up gold so he can take care of you." Blueberry Pete put a big gold nugget in my hand. "He can't wait to see his little girl."

Mama and I stared at the nugget. It didn't sparkle like I thought it would. It was a dark yellow color and very heavy. "Now we won't have to worry about money, Mama."

Mama put her finger to her lips and shook her head. "How can we join my husband?" she asked Blueberry Pete.

"When the ocean freezes, a coach will carry you to Council City," he explained. "Then you'll take a dogsled to our mining camp at Ophir Creek."

I looked out at the big wide ocean. "The ocean freezes?"

"You'll be amazed at what you see up here. It gets so cold, your nose could fall off." Blueberry Pete pretended to pull off my nose.

I looked at Mama. *Is he teasing me?*

Mama laughed. "Mr. Pete, are you coming with us?" she asked.

Blueberry Pete shook his head. "My old bones can't take another cold winter. I'm going to California. But I'll see you in June."

Blueberry Pete took us to the Golden Gate Hotel. Then he said good-bye.

2

By Horse and by Husky

Every morning I woke up and ran to the window. No snow.

Mama kept us busy. We walked up and down the muddy streets of Nome. We looked at all the restaurants and shops. New log buildings were going up every day. Sometimes we watched people panning for gold on the beach.

Nome was much more exciting than Blacktail Gulch.

Just when I couldn't wait another day, the ice on the ocean began to thicken. One morning Nome was covered with snow. The ugly piles of garbage were velvety white mounds. "Soon we'll be with Papa!" I shouted.

"Not a moment too soon," Mama said. Mama had paid for our room and meals with the gold nugget Blueberry Pete had given us. But the money was almost gone.

I crossed my fingers. We just had to get to Papa.

We finally set off in a big wooden coach with six white horses. It sounds like a fairy tale. But the coach wasn't fancy at all. It was made out of coarse plywood and the seats were hard.

All day the coach jolted over the rough ocean ice near the shoreline. All night at the roadhouse, my body ached.

Later the coach moved back onto land. We traveled over the snowy hills. Sometimes the horses got stuck knee-deep in the big drifts. One day it snowed very hard. The horses couldn't see where they were going. The coach barely stopped at the edge of a cliff.

Finally we arrived in Council City. I peered out the coach window at the tents and wooden buildings. A huge man opened the door.

"I'm Big Hans, your papa's partner," he said in a booming voice.

"Where is my husband?" Mama asked. Her voice shook.

"He's at the mine. But don't you worry. I'll have you there in no time."

Papa sure does work hard, I thought, getting out and stretching my legs. *I hope he has time for me.*

Big Hans tucked Mama and me into a sled. He covered us with reindeer

hides to keep us warm. Six huskies
were already harnessed to the front of
the sled.

Big Hans jumped on the runners at
the back of the sled. "Mush!" he yelled.

The dogs raced over the snowy
tundra. My chest hurt so I could hardly
breathe.

Big Hans hollered, "Haw!" The team turned left. Just then a flock of white birds flew in front of the lead dog's nose. The dogs turned right, following the birds. The sled tipped over! I went tumbling into a snowdrift.

Big Hans plucked me up, shook me off, and dropped me back in the sled.

"Oh, what an adventure!" Mama said as the dogs took off running again.

After a while, Big Hans stopped the sled, right in the middle of nowhere. "Home sweet home!" he hollered.

I looked around. Nothing but whiteness.

Then a tall man in a long dark coat seemed to pop up from the snow.

"Papa!" I yelled. I jumped out of the sled and into his arms.

"Klondy, how big you've grown," he said. He put me back down on the ground.

I watched as my handsome papa
kissed my mama. *Papa.* How I loved
that word.

3
The Cabin at Ophir Creek

Papa's whole cabin wasn't any bigger than our living room back in Blacktail Gulch. It had a woodstove, one chair, a tiny table, and a few shelves made out of packing crates. No curtains or pictures to make it pretty.

The next morning the cabin was still dark when I woke up. I heard a sizzling sound. I jumped out of bed and ran over to the stove. Papa was flipping a pancake. When the next one started bubbling, I asked if I could do it. Papa nodded and handed me the spatula.

I stuffed myself with sourdough pancakes topped with maple syrup. The syrup came from a tin in the shape of a log cabin.

It was dark until noon. Then it grew
light outside. This far north the sun
only shone two hours a day during the
winter. Papa, Mama, and I went for
a walk. I had to run to keep up with
Papa's long legs. But I didn't mind.

"See the little fir trees, Klondy?"
Papa asked. He pointed to the hill
behind our cabin. "We can cut one
down for Christmas."

"Oh, Papa," I said. "I can't wait!"

"Show us where you work, Warren,"
Mama said.

We walked on a path by the creek.
I knew we had reached the mine when

I saw huge piles of dirt all around us.

"We have to dig very deep to find the gold." Papa pointed to two small buildings nearby. "The other miners live there. They eat in the mess hall and sleep in the bunkhouse."

"Where do their families live?" Mama asked.

"I'm the lucky one," Papa said, smiling. "Nobody but me has a family here."

I looked at Mama. She looked at me. There were no ladies for Mama to talk to. There were no children for me to play with.

The next day Papa went back to the mine. That evening I scratched the frost off the window and waited for him. He didn't come home by supper or even by bedtime.

"Please let me wait up for Papa," I begged. Mama helped me say my prayers instead.

I lay awake in my bunk, listening for the crunch of his boots. Wolves howled outside the cabin. Mama got up and bolted the door.

In the morning I could smell Papa's pipe tobacco. But his bed was empty.

4

Papa Gets Angry

Life at Ophir Creek was quiet. I missed the busyness of Nome. I missed my friends in Blacktail Gulch. I missed my room at the boardinghouse.

Most days it was too cold to play outside. Mama tried her best to keep me busy inside. We made bread. Mama showed me how to knead the dough and shape it into loaves. I stirred the moose stew that simmered on the stove.

I'd had to leave my toys behind in South Dakota, so Mama made me a rag doll out of Papa's old sock. The doll had buttons for eyes and frizzled sugar sack drawstrings for hair. I named her Maggie and pretended she lived in a fancy dollhouse.

One afternoon Mama decided our cabin was too bare. She opened her trunk and pulled out her petticoats. "Your aunties and I made these back in Sweden. That was before your papa and I were married." I stepped into one and twirled around. The fabric danced in the air.

I looked over at Mama. Tears were sliding down her cheeks. But she took scissors out of her sewing basket. "I have no place to wear these fancy clothes up here. Let's put them to use."

We sewed the lacy material into pillowcases and a tablecloth. When Mama cut curtains from her wedding dress, I couldn't bear to help. I remembered the photo of Mama and Papa on their wedding day. Mama looked so beautiful in her dress.

Mama was quiet when the curtains were done. I wanted her to forget the dresses. "Let's make doughnuts," I said. They were her favorite.

Sizzle, pop, pop. The oil sputtered as the big blobs of dough cooked. They smelled so good. We dipped them in sugar. When I ate one, the sugar left a ring around my mouth.

"May I take some to Papa while they're hot?" I wrapped up a few doughnuts, placed them in a basket, and waited. Mama had never let me go to the mine alone before.

Finally she nodded. "Be careful,"

she said. "And come right home."

I put on my rabbit-fur jacket and my boots made of reindeer hide. Then I followed Papa's trail in the snow along the creek. I wanted to stop and watch the birds and follow the rabbit tracks. But I had to be back by dark.

At the mine, the men hauled up dirt in buckets and dumped it in a heap. Papa pulled up the heaviest loads. He also told the other men what to do.

When he finally saw me, I waved. But Papa didn't wave back. He didn't even smile. Instead, he yelled and shook his finger. "What are you doing

here, Klondy? This is no place for a
little girl!"

My legs felt glued to the ground.
"Go home to your mother," he said. He
turned back to his work. The basket of
doughnuts slipped out of my hands.

When I could finally move my legs, I began to run. With one big step, Big Hans reached out his arm and stopped me. "Don't cry, Klondy. It's dangerous here. Your papa worries you could get hurt."

I broke out of his grip and started running again. I had thought life would be perfect once we joined Papa. But he was always busy. Now he was angry with me.

I burst through the cabin door. "Papa hates me! I'm just a bother to him. I want to go back to South Dakota."

"No. No. Your papa loves you very much," Mama said. She wiped away my tears. "He just thinks that finding lots of gold will make us happy."

"I'd be happy just to see him every night, Mama."

"I know," she said. "I know."

5
Klondy's Christmas

Papa had promised to cut down a
Christmas tree with me. But he never
had time. So Big Hans offered to help
instead. We hiked around, looking for
just the right one. They all seemed so
tiny. I wondered if Papa would have
known where to find a bigger one.

"Klondy, look at those reindeer way

up on the hill!" Big Hans shouted.

"Papa told me they belong to Santa. He says I'll be Santa's first stop." I looked at Big Hans. "I hope Papa will spend Christmas with us," I said quietly.

"I know the other miners will miss their families," Big Hans said.

I thought a minute. "Let's have a party," I said. The idea made me happy for the first time in many days.

Big Hans and I returned with a little tree and a big plan. "All the miners are homesick for their families, Mama. Let's plan a big Christmas Eve party for them. Even Papa will have to stop work early on the twenty-fourth."

Mama and I had a lot to do in three days. We popped corn and strung it. We made ropes from cranberries I dug out of the snow. We baked gingerbread men with curling caps. We practiced Christmas carols.

The night before the party, I barely slept. Mama had wrapped my rag curls so tightly that my head hurt.

When the men left for the mine in the morning, Mama and I snuck the tree into the mess hall. We strung the cranberry and popcorn ropes around it. We hung the gingerbread men and wired thick miners' candles to the branches.

I looked at the tree. Something was missing. Mama flattened out a baking powder tin and cut out a star. I crawled up on the big table and hooked it to the very top.

"I wish the tree were bigger, Mama.
Like the ones back in South Dakota."

"Don't spend your life wishing for
what you don't have, Klondy," she said,
pulling me close. "Learn to be happy
with what you have this very minute."

That evening I put on my red party dress. Mama untied the rags in my hair. Corkscrew curls bounced around my neck. Mama wore her fancy black dress. Her hair was piled high on her head. I couldn't wait to see Papa's face when he entered the mess hall.

When the miners arrived, they cheered and clapped. One of them called out, "Just like Christmas back home, Klondy!"

I hardly recognized the men. They wore clean shirts and had slicked down their hair. Some had even shaved.

I looked around. "Where is Papa?"

"He'll be here any minute now, Klondy," Big Hans told me.

"Why don't we sing a Christmas carol?" Mama suggested. She started the one I liked best.

"Hark! The herald angels sing
Glory to the newborn King. . . ."

We gathered around the tree. The men joined in. Some of them had tears on their cheeks. Just like Mama that day we sewed the curtains.

My eyes swept the room. Where was Papa?

"Peace on earth and mercy mild,
God and sinners reconciled. . . ."

As we sang the last note, I heard sleigh bells. I ran to the window. A sled and six reindeer had stopped outside!

There was a loud thumping on the roof. A pair of boots with turned-up toes popped through the smoke hole in the ceiling. Down dangled two scrawny legs in red woolen underwear.

"Queeck, coom, somebody! Heelp!" a voice called out.

Big Hans jumped up on the table and yanked on the feet. A funny old man fell to the floor. He wore a white parka and a stocking cap. But he didn't look like pictures of Santa I'd seen in books. And he didn't say "ho ho ho" or even "Merry Christmas."

The man dropped a burlap sack at my feet. Then he stomped out the door. Big Hans opened the sack. Out tumbled gold nuggets and bags of gold dust, rabbit and fox furs. I knelt in the furs and touched the gold.

"Oh, Klondy. How generous," said Mama. I looked up. Papa was standing beside her, his arm around her waist.

"Papa!" I cried.

"Merry Christmas, Klondy," he said.

That night I fell asleep with my doll, Maggie, in my arms. The miners had been so happy with the party. But I couldn't help wishing for just one toy.

The smell of Papa's pipe woke me up the next morning. "Klondy! It looks like Santa made another visit."

On the table stood a dollhouse made of the syrup tin. Light shone through its windows. Real smoke

curled up the chimney from a candle
inside.

"Oh, Papa," I said. "A dollhouse!
Just what I've always wanted."

It wasn't big enough for Maggie.
But tomorrow I could carve some tiny
dolls to fit inside. Today I had my papa.

Author's Note

A real girl named Klondy Nelson lived in Ophir Creek, Alaska, one hundred years ago. Eventually her father mined enough gold to buy his family a house in Nome. There Klondy and her little brother, Ophir, raced dogs and went ice fishing with the Inupiaq Eskimos.

Blueberry Pete and Big Hans were lifelong friends of the Nelson family. When Klondy grew up, she raised two children in Alaska. She also wrote a book called *Daughter of the Gold Rush*.